James Driscoll

the Shoe People

P.C. BOOT'S
SURPRISE BEAT

Lesley Young

CARNIVAL

P.C. Boot, the friendliest policeman in Shoe Town, was having breakfast. He was just cracking his hard-boiled egg with his truncheon, when he caught sight of the clock on the wall.

"I'm late," he cried, grabbing his notebook and rushing out of Shoe Town Police Station.

Beat commences 9.09 a.m. he wrote in his notebook.

He had just begun his beat when he spotted a square, white piece of litter.

"Got you!" he said, picking it up. There was a big letter S written on it. Further along the road, P.C. Boot picked up another piece of paper. There was a large U on this piece.

P.C. Boot saw other pieces in front of him, like a sort of trail.

Strange!

If P.C. Boot had been early starting his beat, instead of late, he would have seen a strange sight.

Margot, the beautiful ballerina, had been out first thing in the morning. She had danced through Shoe Town, holding a basket. When she passed Shoe Town Police Station, she had carefully dropped white paper squares in a line on the road.

P.C. Boot picked up eight paper squares, each one with a letter on it. He laid them out, in the order in which they were picked up, on his notebook. They made a word:

SURPRISE

Very strange indeed!

P.C. Boot wrote in his notebook: *SURPRISE found in road.*

Further along his beat, P.C. Boot saw another piece of litter.

There was no message this time. It was just an ordinary piece of litter: a sweet paper from P.C. Boot's favourite chocolates.

Charlie the clown was watching from behind a bush. When he saw P.C. Boot looking at it, he pointed his magic wand.

Flash!

P.C. Boot jumped in amazement. The paper had disappeared, and in its place was a box of chocolates.

As he walked past Puddle Villa, P.C. Boot could see brightly coloured bubbles coming out of the funnel chimney.

"Good morning," shouted Wellington from behind the fence. "Are you having a good day? I hope it's bright, with lots of sunshine!"

"Do you?" asked P.C. Boot in surprise. He knew that Wellington hated the sun. He loved rain and grey skies.

P.C. Boot wrote in his notebook: *Wellington behaving strangely.*

At Tumbledown House, P.C. Boot could see two small figures standing at the gate. It was Hector the hedgehog and Red the squirrel.

"We've been waiting for you," said Hector.

"What is it?" asked P.C. Boot, kindly. "Is it a prickly problem?"

But the two animals held out a gaily wrapped package of nuts for him.

"These are for you. We gathered them specially."

"Don't you need them to see you through the winter?" asked P.C. Boot.

"We have plenty. And we want you to have these today."

As he walked towards Swan Lake Cottage, P.C. Boot could hear someone humming a tune. He strained to hear what it was. It sounded very familiar.

'La, la, la, la – laa – la . . .'

It was Baby Bootee, singing in her pram.

As he reached the house, Margot picked up the baby's dummy and put it firmly in its mouth.

Margot fluttered her eyelashes at him: "Silly child. Doesn't know if it's Easter, Christmas, or someone's birthday . . ."

Sid Slipper was coming down the road.

"I'm having a very strange beat," said P.C. Boot. Perhaps Sid Slipper could help him. He was the wisest person in Shoe Town.

"I can't stop now," said Sid, "I've got an important appointment."

"Oh dear," said P.C. Boot, "I was sure you would know why everything is so strange."

"Sorry," said Sid, "history's more my line – especially special dates!"

P.C. Boot was nearly knocked over by Flip-Flop rushing past him.

"I'm late! I'm late!" she shouted.

"I'll have you for speeding!" said P.C. Boot.

"Don't stop me," yelled Flip-Flop, "I've got to organize some special music. But I'll see you later."

"I'll probably hear you first," said P.C. Boot, and he wrote in his notebook, *Be on the alert for noise nuisance later today.*

A battered red hat was bobbing along behind a hedge. P.C. Boot would have known it anywhere.

"Trampy!" he called out.

Trampy shot into the air, "What a fright you gave me," he said. "I wasn't expecting to see you." As usual, he was clutching a brown paper parcel.

"What have you got there?" asked P.C. Boot.

"Nothing!" said Trampy. "Must rush . . ."

Trampy behaving even more oddly than usual, wrote P.C. Boot.

P.C. Boot had nearly finished his beat. It had been the strangest one he could remember.

As he got near the Police Station, he could see that it looked quite different. There were balloons tied to the doors. The notice board outside had fairy lights round it.

He was looking at these in amazement, when there was a Whoosh! and giant coloured streamers shot out of the chimney. P.C. Boot was almost too astonished to move.

Pushing open the door of the Police Station, P.C. Boot looked in.

He hardly recognized it. All the walls were decorated with paper garlands and silver stars. There was a wonderful smell from orange trees that stood in tubs at each corner.

What was going on? Charlie the clown popped up from behind the desk and pointed his wand at a large, strange shape under a sheet.

P.C. Boot felt that he couldn't take many more surprises . . .

In a flash the sheet disappeared, and there were all P.C. Boot's friends. Everyone he had met on his beat was there, all in their party clothes.

Even Red the squirrel and Hector the hedgehog had party hats on.

Trampy was holding out a special plant he had grown – he must have been hiding it in his brown paper bag.

So that was why everyone had been behaving so strangely! They had been planning this surprise for him. But why?

There was a long table covered with all his favourite food. Gilda Van Der Clog had made him a special cake with flour from her mill. It was in the shape of a notebook, with something written on it.

P.C. Boot went forward to read what it was. At last he understood what was happening. As usual, he had been so busy helping everyone else, that he had forgotten a very special day.

On the cake, in big blue icing letters, P. C. Boot read: HAPPY BIRTHDAY.

Carnival
An imprint of the Children's Division
of the Collins Publishing Group
8 Grafton Street, London W1X 3LA

Published by Carnival 1989

ISBN 0 00 194611 0

Printed & bound in Great Britain by
PURNELL BOOK PRODUCTION LIMITED
a member of BPCC plc